Pain & Wastings

Carrie Mac

Orca soundings

Orca Book Publishers

Library and Archives Canada Cataloguing in Publication

Mac, Carrie, 1975-

Pain & wastings / Carrie Mac.
ISBN 978-1-55143-904-4 (pbk.).--ISBN 978-1-55143-906-8 (bound)

I. Title. II. Title: Pain and wastings.
PS8625.A23P33 2008   jC813'.6   C2007-907177-5

Summary: Fifteen-year-old Ethan must face the truth about his
mother's murder.

First published in the United States, 2008
Library of Congress Control Number: 2007941834

Orca Book Publishers gratefully acknowledges the support for its publishing
programs provided by the following agencies: the Government of Canada
through the Book Publishing Industry Development Program and the Canada
Council for the Arts, and the Province of British Columbia through the BC
Arts Council and the Book Publishing Tax Credit.

Cover design by Teresa Bubela
Cover photography by Getty Images
Author photo by Benjamin Owens

Orca Book Publishers
PO Box 5626 Station B
Victoria, BC Canada
V8R 6S4

Orca Book Publishers
PO Box 468
Custer, WA USA
98240-0468

www.orcabook.com
Printed and bound in Canada.
Printed on 100% PCW recycled paper.

11 10 09 08 • 5 4 3 2 1

For Ian Muir and his sick sense of humor.
And for Reggie...sorry about the jacket.

Chapter One

Tonight we're going to break into Playland, the amusement park across the highway from the group home. It was Harvir's idea. It's raining when we climb out the window, but it stops when we are halfway down the alley.

"The rides won't work," I say as we wait for a break in the traffic. "They turn the power off at night."

"Who cares?" Harvir looks like a cat burglar, all dressed in black. "I'm not interested in the rides. I just want to climb the roller coaster."

"What for?"

"Because it's there. And I want to." He dashes onto the highway. A pickup truck slams on its brakes, swerving to miss him. The driver rolls down his window and yells at Harvir as he drives away. Harvir does a little bhangra dance in the fast lane. "Are you chicken, Ethan?" Horns honk. Headlights flash. A sedan screeches to a stop on the shoulder and a beefy guy gets out, his hands already in fists.

"You chicken, Ethan?" Harvir asks again.

I fix him with a glare. We are always one-upping each other. And I always win. I run right at the sedan and jump on the hood—denting it with a loud metallic crunch—onto the roof and down over the trunk end before the guy even realizes what's happening.

"Sucker!" I flip him the finger, and then Harvir and I scale the retaining wall and make a run for it. Along the off-ramp, across the overpass and into the bushes, where we wait to make sure Sedan Man isn't on our trail.

We are only halfway up the first incline of the old wooden roller coaster when the lights flood on below with a loud buzz.

"Don't move!"

The glare of the lights blinds us. We can't see who it is.

"Just security." Harvir keeps climbing. "Rent-a-cops. Harmless."

"And that?" I start down as the sirens get closer.

"Cops. So?" Harvir shrugs. "If they're going to get us anyway, might as well have some fun with it."

So Harvir keeps climbing up while I start climbing down. Just as I'm about to set foot on the cement, they set the cop dog after me. So of course I run. Who wouldn't with a snarling barking beast of doom coming after you? I dare *you* to stand still.

"Stop!" the dog handler yells. "Or it'll get messy. Don't say I didn't warn you."

Yeah, well I'm a good runner, so I'll take my chances. I hop the low fences that form the lineups for rides; so does the dog. I deke in and out of the concession booths; so does the damned dog. I throw myself halfway up a fence that would get me out of the park, and so does the dog, clamping on to the back of my thigh.

He hangs there, midair, ripping my flesh with his teeth, growling.

"Get it off!" I swat at him with one arm while holding myself up with the other. "Okay! Okay!" I can literally hear my skin rip and the burble of blood as it oozes down my leg. The pain makes me high, and not in a good way.

"Good dog, Smokey. Off!" The dog handler gives the shepherd an old plastic pop bottle and a pat on the head. The dog wags his tail and gnaws on the bottle, swinging it back and forth as if it were a rabbit or a rat. Or my leg.

I ease myself off the fence and collapse on the ground, face-first onto the wet cement. "He bit me!"

"That's the idea," the cop says. He snaps a leash on Smokey and leads him away, the dog trotting proudly while two other cops handcuff me where I lie on the ground.

"I need a goddamn doctor!"

"You hear something?" Cop Numbnuts says.

"Just some foul language that don't get you nowhere," Cop Buttface says.

The pain is so bad I have to grit my teeth to talk. "That's a double negative, idiot."

"I think you've got better things to worry about than my grammar, kid." Cop Buttface pulls on a pair of leather gloves. "Anything in your pockets I should know about? Knives? Drugs? Needles?"

"Screw you. I don't do that crap."

"I'll take that as a no." He digs roughly in my pockets, each jostle sending hot pain shooting down my leg.

"Do something about my leg, jerk-off!" I try twisting to see how bad it is but can't. "It's still bleeding, isn't it? It hurts, man. Do something!"

The cop puts a thoughtful finger to his chin. "Now, why is he so upset?"

"An excellent question." The other cop squats beside me. He shines his flashlight on my leg. "Ouch. Look at this, partner."

"Nasty." Cop Buttface wrinkles his nose. "You can see the muscle and fat and everything. Good thing he didn't go for your balls. They've got a command for that, you know."

The cop radio crackles as Buttface organizes an ambulance.

"Warrants, prior arrests…?" Cop Buttface picks through my wallet and pulls out my ID.

He records the details in his notebook. "Might as well tell me now. We've got some time. They don't hurry for this kind of call."

"I'm going to bleed to death, you pig!"

"Let's start with where you live." Cop Buttface turns the page in his notebook. "You're one of the juvenile delinquents from Harbor House, right?"

"I don't have to tell you anything." I writhe on the ground, the pain like a jackhammer digging into the back of my thigh.

"Suit yourself." Buttface flips his notebook shut. He unwraps a piece of gum and folds it into his mouth. "I got all night."

Chapter Two

A million and a half years later, the ambulance shows up. Buttface is on his fifth piece of gum. He takes it out and flicks it into the bush before he waves the paramedics over.

"What have we got?" One of them drops an enormous first-aid kit dangerously close to my head.

I crane my neck to see who's talking. It's a girl paramedic, or woman, I guess. Good looking enough, but a little old. Fake blond with dark roots, hair pulled up in a ponytail. Tired lines around her eyes. A decent rack. She winks at me. "Looks like you had a run-in with Smokey, huh?"

"What took you so long?" I writhe on the ground, my leg screaming with pain, my front soaking and cold, my wrists chafing against the cuffs. "You stop for donuts or something?"

Everyone shuffles in closer and talks over me. Now all I can see are boots. Two cop pairs, shiny and buffed, and two paramedic pairs, scuffed and dull. The cops are telling the paramedics their version of events. I am not surprised to hear that, on the other side of the amusement park, six cops are waiting for Harvir to decide to come down from the top of the roller coaster. I can hear him whooping and hollering in the distance. They probably think he's high, but he's just whacked out like that for real.

"Hello? Somebody get me the hell off the ground, please?"

"Oh, he said *please*." The girl paramedic squats. Her nametag catches a glint of light. *Holly*. "That's sweet."

The other three all go *awwww*, and then

Buttface adds, "He's learned some manners in the last half hour."

"Up you get." Holly grabs one of my arms while her partner yanks on my other one. "We'll fix you up in the ambulance."

"Ow!" I yell as they set me onto my feet. "You're going to make me walk? What the hell? I need a friggin' stretcher!"

They share a look and both let go at once. I teeter on my one good leg, my hands still cuffed behind me. The hard ground looks a long way down, and I do not want to greet it nose first.

"Sorry," I mumble. "Just don't let me fall, okay?"

Holly's partner—*John*, his nametag says— helps me hop to the ambulance. She climbs in ahead of us and puts a plastic sheet on the cot.

"I don't want you bleeding all over my car." She moves the belts on the cot out of the way as I half crawl up the steps. "Get on."

"Come on," I beg. "Get that jerk cop to take the cuffs off."

She sighs. "What was your name?"

"Ethan."

"A piece of advice, Ethan. Don't piss off

emergency services. Not smart." She pats the yellow sheet. "Now get on and try asking one more time. Nicely."

"Jesus! Ah!" I flop onto the cot, hollering as the pain cuts through my leg. "Please can you get them to take the cuffs off?"

"Sure, since you asked so nice." Holly sends John to get the cop to come in and take off the cuffs.

"Finally." I rub my wrists.

"Sorry, officer. He means *thank you*." Holly pats my head. "Right, sweetheart?"

Buttface settles himself on the bench, his belt creaking, his gun angled down at his hip. "You're welcome."

"See?" With me facedown on the cot, Holly cuts up the leg of my jeans. "We can all be nice."

She tugs my pants away from the dog bite. It takes some effort because the blood and fabric have stuck together. I scream. The cop tells me to be a man. I tell him to go and screw himself. Holly pours something cold and stinging onto the wound. I pass out.

When I come to, all I hear is my name. And then I hear it again. And again.

"Ethan Kirby? You're sure that's his name?"

"That's right." I open my eyes to see the cop check his notes. "Sixteen years old."

"How many sixteen-year-old Ethan Kirbys can there be?" Holly murmurs.

We're driving now. We go over a bump. I wince. Buttface leans over me. His breath is alarmingly rank despite the gum he's chewing.

"Good morning, sunshine." He grins. "Not so much the tough man now, are you?"

"What the hell'd they bring you along for?" I sneer at him. "Do I look like I need a police escort?"

"Policy." Holly bends over me. "What's your middle name?"

"He doesn't have one," the cop says. "Just first and last name on his ID."

"I have one." I open my mouth to say it, but Holly holds up a gloved hand to stop me.

"Don't tell me. I bet I can guess it."

I shake my head. "Not a chance."

We take a corner. Holly grips a hand bar and steadies herself. "What do you want to bet?"

"A hundred bucks." There is no way she can guess my middle name.

"You don't have a hundred bucks," Holly says. "And if you do, you shouldn't."

"Fine then, you think of something. You won't guess it anyway."

We lock eyes for a second. There is something strange about the way she's looking at me, like she knows me, only I've never seen her before in my life. "You're bandaged up now," she says, and the moment passes. "If you want to flip onto your back, you can."

"Okay." I gingerly turn over, keeping the ripped-up leg bent. "God, that hurts!"

"Want a pillow under that?" She pulls one from a cubby and stuffs it into a paper case. "Don't straighten it. It'll kill."

"Yeah." Why is she being so nice? "Thanks."

She tucks the pillow under my knee and then sits on the bench beside the cop. She tugs at her stethoscope and just sort of sits there, staring at me.

John turns his head in the driver's seat and peers at us through the partition. "Almost there."

The chops and static of the ambulance radio sound from the front, mixed in with the classic rock station John has on low. I sit up and look out the window. The people in the cars behind us can't see in, but we can see out. It's raining again. The streetlights slice orange wedges of glow onto the wet roads. The couple in the pickup truck behind us is arguing, their faces twisted in anger. A baby sits on the woman's lap, sucking his thumb and staring up at his parents. He should be in a car seat, and I'm just about to tell the cop he'd do better spending his time writing up people like that rather than babysitting me, but I change my mind, favoring the silence instead.

We pull in to the children's hospital, with its cheery signs and brightly colored emergency room. The last time I was here I'd been picked up, passed out drunk, in the skate park across the street from Harbor House. The time before that for stitches after I got into a fight. Now I'm here for a police dog bite.

I'd rather go to the regular hospital, but

minors have to go to the children's hospital, especially if you're a ward of the state. It's weird to come here for such badass things when most of the patients are just new babies, or little kids playing happily with the toys in the waiting room or clinging tearfully to their parents while they wait to get their boo-boo fixed or fever treated or the marble removed from up their nose.

The cop gets out first. He swaggers in ahead of us to tell them all about my criminal record and to recommend that I have a room to myself so as not to cause trouble or frighten the children. Like I would. In a children's hospital, where bald-headed cancer kids ask you to play snakes and ladders, and busted-up toddlers want you to draw on their casts? I'm not bad. Not *that* bad. I'm not.

Just as Holly is about to jump out and help her partner with the cot, she leans over and says, "I win the bet, you come on a ride-along with me. On a nightshift."

"And if I win?"

"You win, and I'll buy you a new pair of jeans to replace the ones the dog ruined."

"They were expensive."

"And probably stolen, so don't push your luck." She takes off her gloves and we shake hands. "Deal?"

"Deal."

"Mingus." She doesn't smile when she says it. She stares at me hard. "Ethan Mingus Kirby."

I look away, all of my thoughts drying up into one dusty tangle and lodging at the back of my throat.

"I knew your mom."

I glance back. She's still staring. Waiting for me to say something. But I don't know what to say, so I don't say anything at all. I turn my head away.

John opens the back doors. "All set?"

"Sure."

Holly jumps out without another word, and then they wheel me in and the triage nurse starts in with her questions and assumptions. As they transfer me onto a hospital stretcher, Holly doesn't mention the bet again. She doesn't ask me anything else. She doesn't explain herself either. Or tell me how she knew my mom. She just lets me be. Alone and quiet while we wait for the doctor, the sound of babies crying, a cartoon playing on the TV in the lobby, my cop escort snapping his gum, his radio squawking.

Chapter Three

Break-and-enter, mischief, resisting arrest and vandalism. The vandalism is for Sedan Man's car. He went whining to the police about his hood being crunched in, and they didn't have to work too hard to connect the dots.

"What about my damage, huh?" I ask while Marshall, bleary-eyed and yawning on his third back-to-back shift as Harbor House babysitter, tells me about the charges. "What do I get for having the back of my leg ripped out? And my jeans. A total write-off."

Marshall yawns. He's got a mug of coffee in front of him, but he hasn't touched it. "What do you get?" he asks, like he doesn't get the question. And then he repeats it, drawing out each word. "What do you get?"

"For the pain and suffering." I stand up and drop my pants. "Police brutality. For this!"

"Nice underwear," Marshall says. I'm wearing boxers with happy faces on them. "Is that why you never smile? 'Cause your underwear smiles for you?"

"Forty stitches for starters." I do up my belt. "And I think it's infected. And what if I get that flesh-eating disease? We're talking lifetime comp in that case. Lost wages, the full meal deal, man. They pay big-time for police brutality."

"You'll probably just get time in juvie for being an ass." Marshall takes a slow sip of his coffee. He pushes himself out of his chair and stands, clutching the mug to his bony chest. "The officer is coming by after school. With your social worker. Be here."

"My social worker?" I hesitate. "What's Chandra got to do with it?"

"Beats me." Marshall leaves the room with

a shrug and a yawn. "Go to school. Please. I don't want to come pick you up for shoplifting somewhere because I really, really, really want to sleep."

Poor Marshall. I'm not being sarcastic either. I do feel sorry for him. He was up all night with Kelly, who came home tweaked right out. Harbor House policy says he's supposed to take her to the hospital when she's all methed up, but she'd been missing all day and half the night, and he was just glad she came home. He's cool like that. Keeping us out of trouble when he can. As for Kelly, she's asleep upstairs. Finally.

School—if you can call a portable full of losers *school*—is the last place I want to be. It's been a week since the roller-coaster climb. Harvir is already in juvie for who knows how long. School was bearable with Harvir there, but now it's so boring it makes me want to poke Captain's eyes out just to generate some excitement. And I like Captain. As far as teachers go, he's the best one we've had this year. It's April, and he's our third. Last year we went through six. We usually place bets on how long they'll last, but no one's brought up the wager since Captain came at the end of November. No one will say it out loud, but we like him.

Just before English, he comes to the back of the portable, where I'm putting in shelving by the door. He says it's for our shoes, for when it gets really mucky out, but I know it's his way of having me use my math and organizational skills without being obvious. Even though it is kind of obvious. He had Harvir and me plan it all, including a budget for the supplies and everything. Whatever. It's better than working on some stupid workbook.

"Something on your mind?"

"Isn't that your job?" I make a mark on the wall with my pencil. "To put something in there for me?"

He leans against the door. He's huge, probably six and a half feet tall. He makes the portable feel like a dollhouse. He was captain of a minor-league hockey team until he blew his knee. That's why we call him Captain. "Talk to me," he says.

I tell him about the pig (cop) and sow (social worker) coming after school. He takes it in stride. He's never fazed by the crap we get up to.

"You can't be surprised," he says when I pause. "You knew something was going to come of it."

"Silly me. I thought my leg being shredded by a vicious dog was enough."

Captain shrugs. "I guess not."

"Can you write me a letter?" I play with the tape measure, not sure if this'll go over well. "Tell them how good I'm doing and everything? Tell them it would be disruptive to my education if I have to go to juvie?"

"I could just photocopy the other three I've written you…" Captain squints at the big calendar on the far wall, "…in the last six weeks. How about that?"

I let the measuring tape snap back into the casing. "It'd have to be a new one."

"No can do this time." Captain shakes his head. "Got to draw the line somewhere, buddy."

"How about you draw the line the next time I ask?"

He levels me with That Look. We've all got it from him enough to know it. That look that says, I know you're smarter than what you've *a)* just done or *b)* just said.

"How about you finish up here and join us for English?"

"Fine." I chuck the hammer and level into the toolbox. "Thanks for nothing."

"Take it easy, Ethan." Captain claps a hand on my shoulder as he heads for his desk.

I bristle. "Don't touch me." It comes out a low growl, but he hears every word. I'm holding the toolbox in one hand, the handle hard in my clenched fist. I let it drop. It bangs to the floor and spills open, sending tools clanking onto the tiles. The paper bag of nails rips open, an army of them skittering across the floor.

"Pick them up. Every single one of them, Ethan. Now."

I glance at the nails and then at the door. Get on my hands and knees in front of everybody while they take turns reading out loud from *The Lord of the Flies*, or take off and have the afternoon to myself?

"You pick them up!" I shout. Thankfully, Captain is far enough away from the door that I can get out before he can stop me. I hobble down the stairs and run-limp as fast as I can with my one bad leg slowing me down.

I turn back at the parking lot to see if Captain's following. He's not. He's standing on the top stair, arms folded, just watching me.

Chapter Four

It's dark when I finally head back to Harbor House. Marshall is still there. He was off at five, but his relief hasn't shown up yet. He points a painted fingernail at me. Still with the yawns, still with the mug of coffee.

"You blew it." He's slouched in an easy chair in the living room, watching some stupid reality TV show about fat celebrities. "Chandra wants you to call her."

"Nice manicure."

"Kelly," he flutters his fingers. "It's called

Pink Pom-Poms. She does a good job. Where were you?"

"I got hung up."

Marshall twists his head over one shoulder to look at me. "Oh yeah?"

"I had to stay late at school."

"That reminds me." He turns back to his show. "Captain called too. He says if you have perfect attendance for the next two weeks, he'll pretend today never happened."

Moving right along to safer topics...I ask, "Where is everybody?"

"Pizza night," he says with a dismissive flap of his hand. "With that churchy group who thinks all it takes to make you ruffians a bunch of shining lights of God is a couple of large pies with extra cheese and a *G*-rated comedy."

"Yeah." I force a laugh. "Suckers." I back out of the front hall, hoping to make it to the stairs without him remembering all my trespasses, so to speak.

"Hey," Marshall calls from the living room. "Some paramedic showed up with the cop and Chandra. She the one from that night?"

This stops me in my tracks. *Ethan Mingus Kirby. I knew your mother.*

My mouth goes dry. The room spins into darkness.

I am six. I've been crying for so long I'm hoarse. I peed my pajamas because I don't want to go into the bathroom. They're my favorite pajamas, with red fire engines and Dalmatian dogs.

I grip the banister and pull myself back into the moment. I breathe in through my mouth and exhale slowly through my mouth, like Chandra tells me to do when this happens.

I clear my throat. "Is her name Holly?"

"Yeah." From the hallway I can hear Marshall flipping the channels.

"Then yeah, she was the one that night."

"She wanted me to give you a message…" The news, a game show, country music. He parks it on a tattoo of gunfire. Tires screech. A woman screams. "She says you owe her. Something about a bet?"

Chapter Five

I called Chandra. She's coming today. With the cop. And Holly. They show up all at once and give the neighbors a reason to gawk. Cop car, ambulance and Chandra's 1968 Ford Mustang with the flames airbrushed above the wheel wells. She really is the best sow to have, if you have to have one. She's been mine since I was eight.

"How's the leg?" Holly says as she climbs down from the ambulance. Her partner waves from the driver's seat but doesn't get out.

"Fine." I turn to Chandra. "What's she doing here?"

"Be glad she's here." Chandra grabs my file from the mess of paperwork on her front seat. "She might just be your best friend."

"What do you mean?" I scowl at the cop as he gets out of his car. He's not one of the two from the other night. This one is younger, with spiky black hair and a tattoo peeking out from his shirtsleeve. He drove up in one of those souped-up cop cars they take to the schools when they give lectures about the dangers of street racing and drug addiction. Youth Liaison Officer. The laziest kind of cop.

"Put on the kettle, Ethan." Chandra pushes past me and heads for the kitchen table, where she spreads my file out in front of her. "Let's get started."

Chandra and Holly drink tea. The cop doesn't drink anything. Marshall nurses his constant cup of coffee. I have a glass of water in front of me, but I haven't taken a sip. I want to, but I feel like if I make even the slightest motion, things will shift badly. So I sit very, very still while Holly presents me with her proposal. It sounds too good to be true.

"Instead of criminal charges, you come with me, as a ride-along, for a block of shifts."

"He's got school," Marshall says.

"We'll take care of that." Chandra glances around the kitchen, clearly approving of its cleanliness. She loves clean. So does Marshall, which is one of the reasons they like each other so much. "The shifts can count toward his Career Prep hours. I already checked with his teacher."

I'll get out of school, with permission, because I broke the law? I shift my eyes to the cop. There has to be a catch, and he's likely to deliver it. But he's not even listening. He's looking at his cell phone. He smiles at it and starts a text message, using his thumbs. He never even looks up.

"That's two nights, two days," Holly's saying. "Twelve hours each. Six to six."

I have a million questions, like, will the charges totally disappear? Do I get to sleep on the nightshifts? Do I have to wear one of their stupid polyester uniforms? Will I have to actually touch puke or blood? And is she going to mention my mom? Because if I'm trapped with Holly in the back of an ambulance for forty-eight hours, she better not. I'll pound her face in and then she'll be needing her own ambulance.

That makes me smile. A paramedic needing an ambulance.

"What is it?" Chandra's mouth is set in a frown. "This amuses you, Ethan?"

I shake my head.

"Then you'll agree to it?"

"Come on, Chandra." I look at the ceiling. "You got candid cameras somewhere? This is some kind of a joke? You honestly expect me to believe that you will let me out of school to go hang out on an ambulance for four days instead of being charged and going to juvie?"

"You don't agree then." Chandra tidies her papers, chopping them on the table to square the edges. "Fine. Officer Omar will process you downtown. You can go with him."

Officer Omar looks up now, surprised. "What?"

"Wait!" I put my hands up in protest. "No, I'll do it."

Chandra stands. "I don't have time for your sarcasm, Ethan."

"I'm sorry. Of course I'll do it. It just seems too easy, you know? Like I'm being set up."

"Perhaps it is difficult to believe that someone wants to offer you a helping hand." Chandra purses her lips in that way that makes her look matronly, despite her fashionable clothes and smart haircut. "But Holly is doing just that. I suggest you take her up on the offer. Concessions are being made for you, Ethan. Holly has even managed to get approval for you to do this despite your criminal record. She had to go to her superintendent for special permission. This is a rare opportunity for someone like you. Don't be flippant about it. Unless you really want to go hang out with Harvir for a while."

"No." I look at Holly. She doesn't smile at me. She's got wrinkles around her mouth. Probably a smoker. Her expression is even. She's not giving anything away. I have all kinds of ideas about how she might've known my mother, but I can't settle on the one I want to believe. And I don't want to ask her. And she better not bring it up.

Chapter Six

The first shift is a dayshift. Chandra comes and picks me up. When I get in the car she gives me a disapproving shake of her head.

"I told you to dress nicely. That means no sneakers." She hands me a bag from the thrift store. "No jeans. Change into this."

I look in the bag. Navy blue slacks. And a white button-up shirt.

"And wear the boots we got you for those community service hours you did at the recycling depot."

I stare at her.

"You still have them?" she asks.

"Yeah. You want me to wear this crap?"

"You *will* wear it, and you will *not* be argumentative for me or Holly. Not at all. Or the deal is off and you go to juvie. And I'll make sure you're going in just as Harvir is coming out, so don't think for one minute that you two would get a chance to even say hello. I told you to go get changed, so go. And put on a white undershirt."

I go back inside and get into the clothes. It's all a little big and smells of the thrift store, stale and slightly sweet. Chandra's gotten me a belt too, a thin one with a dainty gold buckle that might suit an airline steward or a pedophile who likes to watch children play in the park.

Chandra honks her horn. I yank out the belt, dig around in the mess on the floor at the foot of my bed, find my studded belt and jab it through the loops as I run down the stairs.

"That's a big improvement." Chandra grins as I get in. "You look sharp. That's a much better belt."

"I look like a waiter in a really cheap restaurant." I pluck at the collar of the shirt.

It's been washed so many times you can practically see right through. "Good call on the undershirt."

I don't know where I thought the ambulance station would be, but I did not imagine it would be right downtown. Smack dab in the heart of the notorious Downtown Eastside. Ten square blocks of drugs and prostitutes and poverty and violence. When Chandra turns onto Hastings, I speak up.

"Where exactly is it?"

"Cordova and Heatley."

That's only a couple of blocks from Main and Hastings, which is called Pain and Wastings for a reason. Hell, a million good reasons.

"Were you going to tell me that? Ever?"

Chandra takes a hand off the wheel to find some music on the radio. "Was I supposed to?"

"You've read my file."

"Uh-huh." She cranks up the radio. Jazz. It would be. "So?"

There are three bay doors, and one of them is opening as we pull up. An ambulance rolls out, with Holly and John in front. John turns on all the emergency lights as Holly rolls down the window.

"You're late! Get in!"

I glance at my watch. It is one minute past six. Chandra thrusts a paper bag at me.

"Your lunch. Go!"

I fumble my way out of Chandra's car and into the side door of the ambulance, not even getting into the jump seat before John peels onto the street and starts the sirens up. There is a small square cutout in the wall that separates the front from the back. The only place for a third person is back here, so I can't see where we're headed. All I can see is out the back window, as the traffic merges into the lanes behind us after we pass.

"Where are we going?"

As an answer, Holly hands me a laminated tag with the ambulance service logo on it and *Observer* in big letters.

"Clip that to your shirt pocket. Don't touch anything, don't talk to anyone, don't puke and don't faint."

"Where are we going?" I can hear the panic in my voice. It's the sirens, and the speed. I twist sideways in the seat and crane my neck so I can peek out the front. It's a weekday and busy already. We're cutting right down the middle of the street, spreading the traffic to two sides as we go. John lays on the horn whenever someone doesn't get out of his way fast enough. The radio is on, AC/DC competing with the siren and John's steady commentary about stupid drivers.

Holly is writing something on a form on a clipboard in her lap. She's got the map book open and checks it now.

"Left at the next street," she says, hardly looking up.

"Where the hell are we going?" I practically scream.

John tosses Holly a dirty look. I bet he does not want me here at all. Holly finishes writing on her form. She checks the map again as we veer to the left, onto a side street. "Right at Maple," she says to John, and then she finally turns to me, just as John cuts the siren and throws the ambulance into park. "Sudden death."

We're led into a housing project, where an obese woman in a stained nightie is pacing in front of the door, a cigarette in each hand, one lit, one waiting to be lit.

"It's my mom!" She points with the lit cigarette. "Up there!"

"Put these on." Holly hands me a pair of latex gloves. "Follow me."

"No way!" I back against the railing.

"For Christ's sake," John says as he shoves me ahead of him into the stinking apartment. "Don't be such a pussy!"

"My mom!" the woman yells behind us. "Go help her!"

I'm sandwiched between John and Holly, with nowhere to go but up the stairs. We congregate in the tiny hallway at the top.

"Stick with me," Holly says. "Carry the jump kit." She points to their bag of first-aid gear, which weighs at least seventy pounds. John opens the first door and sees nothing. Same with the second. Holly turns in to the bathroom.

"In here."

An elderly woman is sitting on the toilet, her slacks bunched around her ankles. An overwhelming stench hits us as we get closer.

The old lady is leaning forward, sort of hugging her knees.

"Ma'am?" Holly moves the woman's lank gray hair out of the way and puts a finger to her neck. "No pulse, John."

"Do something!" I yell. The old lady doesn't look dead. She looks like she was taking a dump and decided to have a snooze. Holly lifts up the old lady's blouse and puts her stethoscope to her back. "No heart sounds."

"Can't you guys give her CPR or something?"

"Sure, Ethan. Great idea." John leans in the doorway. "Why don't you help her onto the floor?"

Without another thought, I grab the old lady's bony shoulders and pull. She comes forward fixed in her sitting position. Rigor mortis. I let go with a horrified shove. The old woman teeters back onto the toilet and then tips to the left, the bathroom counter sparing her an ugly tumble to the floor.

John laughs. "See the blood pooled in the skin where she's been sitting?"

The wrinkly flesh of her butt is purple and blotchy.

"She's been dead a while. There's no CPR in the world would bring her back."

Holly steers me back into the hall. "Why don't you go wait outside?"

I turn a foggy circle, knowing the stairs are right in front of me, but not knowing how to work my feet to take a step forward, let alone navigate the stairs without falling.

"Mommy?" I shake her. Nothing. "Mommy? Wake up!" I sit beside her on the cold bathroom floor for a while, eating crackers out of the box, dipping my fingers into the peanut butter jar. When I'm full, I try to wake her up again. I want her to go get some milk. There's none in the fridge. In fact, there's nothing left in the fridge. I want her to wake up so we can go to the store together. I push with all of my kid might, and she budges, but all wrong. All stiff and hard. Not floppy, like when she's been like this before.

Chapter Seven

I don't remember going back to the ambulance, but that's where Holly finds me when they're finally ready to go. They had to wait for the police to come before they could leave. I don't know how much time has passed. I've just been sitting in the back of the ambulance with the cot lights off, thankful for the cool dark quiet.

"Ready to go, kiddo?" Holly secures the oxygen tank back in its place.

"What the hell are you trying to prove?"

She smiles at me. A generic smile that gives

nothing away. "If you don't cinch it tight, it rattles when we drive."

I meant what is she trying to prove by dragging me along? I meant what is she trying to prove by making me see stuff that brings it all back? I meant what the hell is she trying to prove—that I'm not the badass everyone thinks I am? And who the hell is she? And what does she know about my mother?

She pats the tank. "Snug as a bug in a rug."

I glare at her.

"You want to talk about the call?"

"The call?" I ratchet my glare up a notch.

"The dead lady." John's at the back door, putting away the jump kit. "The call."

"No." I let him in on the glare too. "I do not want to talk about 'the call.'"

"Okay, then," Holly says. "Put your seat belt on."

I put my seat belt on. John and Holly climb in the front.

"Chinese food?" John says, even though it's barely seven in the morning now.

"I'm more in the mood for a hamburger, I

think." Holly turns in her seat. "What do you feel like eating, Ethan?"

"I don't."

"First dead person, kid?" John says as he pulls the ambulance into traffic.

I decide not to answer him, because I don't want to get into it. I eye Holly, but she's not answering for me. How much does she know?

The silence stretches out awkwardly. "Well," John glances in the rearview mirror. His expression is generous for once, and not patronizing. "Either way. If you want to talk about it, we're here."

Chapter Eight

That first shift is the longest twelve hours ever.
We only get back to the station twice, for less
than twenty minutes each time. We do thirteen
calls, all in the Downtown Eastside, my old
neighborhood. I haven't really spent any time
there since I was little, but it hasn't changed
much. Drug dealers, hookers, junkies, crazies,
bums, winos, street kids, johns and pimps.
Pawnshops selling stolen goods, seedy bars with
rat-hole rooms for rent upstairs, twenty-four-hour
porn shops and convenience stores with buzzing

fluorescent lights, storekeepers with baseball bats and tall cans of mace behind the counter. Every alley reeks of piss and festering garbage, each shadowed doorway has a drug deal going on or someone shooting up or a pile of cardboard and blankets hiding someone trying to sleep.

When we're finally done, Holly offers to drive me back to Harbor House. We get into her car and turn onto Hastings without saying a word. Neither of us says anything until we're well out of the Downtown Eastside.

"You okay?" she says without looking at me.

"Sure." I keep my glance trained out the window.

"Mind if I smoke?"

"Nope."

She lights up. The cigarette lasts until we pull up in front of Harbor House. She tosses the butt out the window as I get out. "See you tomorrow?"

"Yup." I stand at the curb and watch her drive away. Her car complains every time she shifts gears. It needs a new clutch. I thought about offering to do it for her, because we learned how last year in shop and I was pretty good at it. I've done three since. I was going to tell her that when we're done the four shifts she should leave her car with me at the school garage and I'd put it in for her, if she paid for the parts. But then I was afraid that if we started talking, she might bring up my mother, so I didn't mention the clutch at all.

Inside, everyone is home. Nikki, Tyrone, Stinky, Doob and Kelly. Mostly we ignore each other, but tonight Kelly has nothing but questions.

"Did you see anything gross?" she asks as we set the table for Marshall's famous frozen lasagna and bagged salad. "Like an amputated arm?"

I lay out forks and knives, and she follows me with plates and napkins.

"Or, like, a nasty crash or something?"

She's following way too close. I can smell her perfume. "Are you on something?" I ask, my voice low so Marshall can't hear me.

Right away with that wounded look she has perfected. "Screw you, Ethan. I was trying to be nice. I was interested, that's all."

"Interested, huh?"

"Yeah! Interested, you jerk!" She's shouting now. So much for not getting Marshall's attention.

"Whoa, hold up there, princess party-pooper," he says.

"What the hell?" Kelly throws a plate to the floor, where it clatters. Places like this always invest in plastic plates and cups for times just like this one.

"Peace," Doob interjects. You can imagine how he got the nickname. He arranges his considerable bulk on one of the kitchen chairs and puts his hands into prayer formation under his chin. "Let us give thanks and feast as brothers and sisters."

"You can be the sister," Stinky says as he switches the cup at Doob's place with his smaller one.

"That's sweet." Kelly picks up the plate from the floor because if she didn't, Marshall wouldn't let her eat until she did anyway. "Really sweet, to get totally dumped on for trying to be nice." She sits down and glares at me. "That's right, Ethan. I was trying to be *nice*."

"Sorry, I couldn't tell." I shrink a little as she

lifts her plate, like she might lob it at me like a Frisbee.

"Psych," she says and sets it down. "Loser."

"Junkie."

"Orphan."

"Throwaway."

"Lasagna?" Marshall lets the pan drop heavily onto the table. Stinky grabs the serving spoon and helps himself to what would be three portions for most of mankind. We hand him our plates and he slops spoonfuls on each one. We dig in. Stinky, Kelly, mute little Nikki, Tyrone muttering to himself, Marshall, and Doob, who takes his plate back with earnest words of thanks.

"Shove it," Stinky says with his mouth full.

"How was your ride-along?" Marshall says in one of his attempts at engaging us in meaningful conversation around the dinner table.

"Didn't you notice?" Kelly says. "He obviously doesn't want to talk about it."

"Thank you, Kelly." I grin at her. "Tyrone," I say, "how about you tell us about the bomb plot the voices inside your head are organizing?"

Tyrone clutches his fork and knife in his fists and holds them out to me. He tilts the knife in my direction and gives me a menacing look. "Not funny."

"All right then." I raise my hands in a truce. "Moving right along...Marshall, how's your boyfriend?"

"The one I never see?" Marshall moves the watery pasta around his plate. "He's just great."

"Nikki?"

She lifts her eyes. She's caked the black eye makeup on extra thick today, and with the white face powder and red lipstick, she really does look like a vampire. She has two piercings in her bottom lip meant to look like fangs, matching little hoops with one blood-red bead closing each. And they do look like fangs. She curls her lip at me and says nothing.

"Well, I saw a dead woman stuck to a toilet," I say. But it's too late. Everyone is spaced out, miserably forking the food to their mouths, each of them daydreaming of where they'd rather be. Me included, although I don't know where that'd be. I actually like this place. It's better than a foster home, and Marshall is as good as it gets when it comes to the adult version of the species, even if he is gay, which is gross. Anyhow, no one is interested in my dead lady, so I go ahead and finish my supper without another word. We are a table of dysfunctional monks, with our silence the only thing keeping the peace.

Doob is blissful, thankful for the calm. He eats with a smile on his face. Sometimes I envy him. He's always happy, even if it's chemically induced at times. But he never seems to be bothered by anything. Even when he was shipped here after three years in one of the seediest foster homes, known to kids citywide, where the rumors include the little kids being locked in cages at night and the older ones being pimped out, he gave the foster mom a hug goodbye when she dropped him off. He wouldn't say a bad word about her when we bugged him for details. "She tries her best," he'd say, or "We are all children of the universe, even Mrs. Medwid."

Not me. Everything gets to me. Sometimes I think I might be crazy, like Tyrone, because I can't let things go. I go over and over things in my head until I want to bash it against the wall just to get some peace. Like my mom.

I'd been better for a while, but now she's all I can think about, ever since Holly mentioned her back on the night the dog ripped my leg apart. And I've had a headache ever since too. And I feel panicky all the time, like any minute I might scream at the top of my lungs and bust through the front door and start running. And keep running until I collapse. That'd feel good, actually. Way better than this constant dread I'm feeling now.

Chapter Nine

That night in bed, I toss and turn and think I probably won't sleep a wink. To keep my mind off my mom, I go over all the things I saw on the ambulance, playing them like commercials in my head, short noisy bursts of color and sound. I'm too wired to sleep. When I do get sleepy, my thoughts turn to my mom, so I pinch myself awake again. At some point, sleep gets the better of me, because the next thing I know the alarm is going off.

Chandra drops me off at the station after telling me that I should've thought to wash my uniform. I tell her it's not a uniform.

"You know what I mean."

"It's not too bad." The pits kind of stink, and there's a red streak from the pasta sauce.

"It's disrespectful."

"It wasn't my laundry day." This is true.

"I don't care."

I would keep going, giving her a hard time, but we're heading back into the Downtown Eastside, and the panic is back in full. I take a deep breath and let it out slowly. My fingers drum on my knee, the other hand clutches the door.

"You okay?"

"Sure." My voice has flattened in the space of three blocks. It's not even 6:00 AM, but the sad, strung-out hookers are on the corners already. Do they have children? Do they have a home? Of any kind? When my mom worked the stroll, she'd lock me in our room with anything sharp stashed away up high. She'd leave me a box of crackers and a stack of cheese slices and a sippy cup of juice and tell me to watch TV until she got back. Now I wonder where she went with her johns when she didn't bring them back to the room. The back of their car? A hotel room somewhere? A flophouse? I don't know.

A few times she brought me along when she went, usually when someone found out I was left alone and called social services on her. Then we'd move to another bug-infested room and she'd take me along for a while, tucking me in warehouse doorways with a backpack full of crayons and coloring books and getting another girl to keep an eye on me for the twenty minutes or so she'd be gone at a time.

We're just around the corner from the station now. There's a man lurching into an alley, his heroin shuffle like a palsy. And another guy sprawled across the doorway to a boarded-up Chinese laundry, intently fishing for a vein. The cops don't care. Even if they did go after every junkie down here, it wouldn't matter. New ones would fill the spaces so fast with the same drawn faces and empty lives that you'd never even notice there was a gap.

Chapter Ten

Holly and John are stretched out on the couches with the morning news on the TV. There are four ambulances stationed here, and they're all in. That makes eight paramedics sharing one very small common room, plus me. There are three couches, two easy chairs and a dining table with office chairs pulled around it. I take one of these. Holly and John don't even say hello. Holly just lifts a hand in response to my greeting and then folds her arms and lets her chin fall to her chest and is asleep again in seconds. I sit there, watching the cheerful banter of the hair-sprayed TV crew, hoping we go out soon.

An hour passes. Two cars have gone out. Another hour passes. The morning news is still on. I've watched the same headlines three times now. Every time the hotline rings with a call, I leap out of my seat, but there's some order to the cars that I don't understand, and so far we haven't gone anywhere. John is snoring. Holly's mouth is open, and with each breath she lets out a little wheeze. The phone rings. John leaps up, wide awake in a nanosecond, and grabs the red phone. He announces his crew number and starts writing on a little pad.

He hangs up and hands the pad to Holly, who is already standing at the bay door. I missed that. She went from sound asleep to ready to rock in seconds. She glances at the paper.

"Code three," she says to me as I push myself out of the chair. Code three means serious. I learned that the day before. Code three means lights and sirens. It also means we get there and it's usually not a big deal, but still, it's pretty exciting.

"What for?" I follow them to the car.

John flips on the lights and pulls out of the bay.

"Short of breath," Holly says. "Don't get your hopes up."

"Yeah." John punches the sirens on and pulls out against traffic. "He's a frequent flyer."

Harold has chronic pneumonia. In addition to hepatitis C, HIV, and diabetes that's so bad his left foot is scheduled for amputation. While we're loading him up, he horks up great gobs of dark yellow phlegm into an old tobacco tin. I gag every time. Even if I look away, there's the sound of it as it lands with a ping in the tin. And the man stinks worse than anyone I've ever met. He smells of sweat and cigarettes and dirty clothes. By the looks of it, he only has the outfit he's got on—brown slacks with a rope for a belt, a too-small shirt with countless stains and four buttons missing, and a polyester cardigan dotted with singe holes from where he probably fell asleep with one of his hand-rolled cigarettes still burning.

It's a tight fit getting the stretcher into his room above the Dodson Hotel. It's not like a real hotel. More a rooming house. My mom and

I lived here once. Room 340. It faced the back, overlooking the alley. We had a cat. I was really little, maybe three or four. My mom only left me alone when Mrs. Charlie across the hall was gone to visit her grandbabies. Usually I stayed with her, and we played tic-tac-toe and watched game shows on her tiny black-and-white TV. She crocheted washcloths, giving them out to everyone in the building. Thinking about it now, did she think that would make people like Harold wash?

I haven't thought about Mrs. Charlie in a long time. She'd talk about Mr. Charlie, especially if she'd had a beer or two. He worked in the diamond mines up north. They had eleven children and ran a trapline year-round. How they ended up down here, I don't know. But Mr. Charlie died of liver failure, so that gives you an idea.

"Where you going, Mommy?" I am sleepy. We played at the park all day. It's not dark out yet, but my eyes are droopy.

"You're going to Mrs. Charlie's for a while." She rummages around, packing a bag for me. Teddy bear, toothbrush, change of clothes. Jazz

is playing on the tape deck. Charles Mingus. The album is called Mingus Ah Um. *I love the diddly bits. I'm four. It was my birthday the day before. The leftover cake sits in its bakery box on the windowsill. It has a music note on it because I love music. Especially jazz, although I don't know that. I just love the tapes she plays when she's getting ready to go out, or when she's sad and stays in bed all day reading picturebooks from the library to me.*

We're backing up to the hospital. Holly is staring at me.

"Hey," she says.

How'd we get here? The last thing I remember was stuffing myself into the tiny elevator at the Dodson. Harold is still hacking up garbage, but Holly's given him a barf bag to hork into. He grins at me, teeth yellowed, gums red.

"She was talking to you…" Cough, cough, hork. "…And you was a million miles away on some other planet." Cough, hork, spit.

He is sweating his stink all over the back of the ambulance. Holly catches me grimacing. Instead of asking me where I went, which is what people usually do when I blank out like that, she kindly ignores it and says instead, "Grab his cane, would you?"

As we wheel him in, the sounds of the bustling emergency department are muffled to me. My head is clattering with thoughts. Chandra used to think I had epilepsy. She figured when I blanked out like that it was a kind of seizure. She had me tested, but nothing showed up.

"It's psychological," she pronounced. I was about ten and wasn't sure what that word meant. I only knew that I'd lose great stretches of time, and when I came to, I was often covered in sweat and breathing hard. She explained what *psychological* was and told me I'd be going to an art therapist once a week from then on.

My foster mother at the time thought art therapy was a stupid idea. I can't remember her name, but I can remember her voice, deep and hoarse like a man's. "Sounds retarded to me," she'd said when she dropped me off at my first session. Even in the hallway, I loved it already. Windows lined one side, letting in bright spring sunshine and lighting up the opposite wall, which was plastered, floor to ceiling, with art. My foster mom yanked me along as I lagged behind, looking at the dragons and sailboats, houses and happy-face suns, dark clouds and lightning bolts and handprints forming colorful flowers. "Stuff for dimwits. You should fit right in, Evan." And I remember that, that she could never get my name right.

Holly waits in line behind the other paramedics to talk to the triage nurse, who looks down her glasses at each of them like a librarian. Holly's chatting with the paramedic in front of her. We saw him a couple of times yesterday. They're laughing and smiling. I lean against the shelving that holds every size and kind of disposable glove you could ever want. Part of me wants to march over there and ask Holly how she knew my mom well enough to know my middle name. I should just get it over with. The rest of me wants to phone Chandra up right now and tell her I'll take juvie over this excruciating trip down memory lane anytime. If she asks my reason, I'll say, "It's *psychological*, Chandra. Get it?"

Chapter Eleven

Kelly tries again with the questions that night, but her approach is better. It's after dinner, and we're in the basement, playing pool. Tyrone came down too, but he's sitting on the washing machine in the corner, in the dark, doing his schizo thing. I don't like hanging out with him, and especially not lately, when my own sanity is in question, but I'm not like Stinky, who's always telling Tyrone to piss off. So long as he keeps his crazies to himself, I don't mind him.

"I am really interested, Ethan." Kelly lines

up her shot. "Maybe I want to be a paramedic, how do you know?"

I bounce my pool cue on my shoe and bite back the scathing remarks I could fire at her. She reads my silence and straightens up without making the shot. "At least I can say I'm trying to stay clean this time. I really am."

"I didn't say you weren't."

"Didn't *say* so." She bends to take the shot, revealing that wedge at the small of her back that is so sexy on a girl. Harvir calls it the ink spot because so many girls get tattoos there. She has one too, a buxom angel kneeling, or it might be a fairy. Either way, she has wings stretching out to the dimples above each butt cheek. I feel myself getting hard. This is bad. I step closer to the table to hide the evidence.

Kelly draws back her elbow, pulling her hand along the thicker part of the cue. "But I get it." She pops the shot, sending the ball straight into the pocket. When Kelly first came three months ago, we all learned very quickly not to bet against her at pool. She's by far the shark of the house.

"Okay," I say. "What do you want to know?"

She backs away from the table and props herself up with her cue. She juts one hip out just a little. Why didn't I ever think she was hot before? Why now? And why right this very minute? I try to buy myself some time and distraction by indulging her little Q & A.

"I don't know." She shrugs. "Everything, I guess."

I start to tell her about the guy we picked up in his car, down by the shipyards, who tried to shoot himself in the head but only managed to take off his ear.

"Holly had me look for it, in case they could sew it back on." It's safe to line up my shot now, thankfully. "But there was only bits, like hamburger, and a lobe."

"Did it have an earring?"

"Yeah, actually it did." It was a clear shot, but I miss anyway. "A gold stud."

"What'd you do with it?"

"The lobe?"

"The earring."

"You want to know what I did with the

earring?" I smile at her. She grins back. She's
wearing a short black skirt that sits low on her
hips, and a tight black tank top. I've always
thought she had great tits, perfect firm little
handfuls, but tonight they look especially
enticing. I glance down at her fuzzy rabbit
slippers, hoping those will take my mind off other
things. "I tell you I was rooting around this guy's
car for his ear, and you want to know what I did
with the earring?"

"Yeah. So?"

"You'd make a great paramedic, Kelly."

Her grin widens to show her teeth, mostly
rotten from all the meth she's done and the
sugar it makes you crave. There goes any risk
for another hard-on. "You think?"

"Sure." I slide right into the safe territory as
she circles the table, assessing the game. "You're
not squeamish, and you have a sick sense of
humor and a weird fascination with stuff like
what they do with the jewelry from blown-off
body parts."

"Thanks, Ethan. That might just be the
sweetest thing anyone's ever said to me." She
calls the shot and then nails it, sending two balls

into opposite corner pockets. "So, what'd you do with the earring?"

Tyrone skulks by us and up the stairs without a word. I tell Kelly that we rinsed the lobe—earring still in place—with saline and wrapped it in gauze in case they could do anything with the tissue at the hospital.

"Huh." She's propping herself up with her cue again. I eye the table, shopping for the easiest shot. "I would've stolen it," she says.

Chapter Twelve

I get to sleep in the next day because Holly and John work the nightshift next. Holly told me to sleep in as late as I could or get up early and have a nap before I have to meet them at 6:00 PM. I choose the sleep-in option and manage not to wake up until almost noon. The house is quiet as I get into the shower. After, I put my pajama bottoms on, thinking I'll get dressed when I have to go. I collect my "uniform" and some other laundry from the heap I'm building on Harvir's bed—seeing as he's not around to object—and head down to the basement. The pool table is neatly racked up and waiting for a new game. Kelly always leaves it like that when she finishes playing.

I put the laundry in and go back up to find something to eat. Kelly is sitting at the kitchen table, doing the crossword that comes in the paper. She looks up. "Thought you might want some company."

I am suddenly acutely aware of the seven chest hairs I was so proud of until this very moment. I shuffle into a chair, wishing I'd put on a T-shirt.

"I have a plan." Kelly sets aside the paper and lays her hands on the table. "We can go hang out downtown until you have to be at the station. I can get us into the movie theater for free."

"So long as it doesn't involve either of us giving anyone a blow job, I'm in." And then I realize what I've just said, and that if it involved her giving *me* a blow job, I wouldn't mind at all. Of course, my cheeks go very, very red. I leap up from the table and fling open the fridge and stick my head in there, pretending to look for something to eat until it passes.

"No." Kelly is suddenly beside me at the fridge. She puts a hand on my bare back. I swear that single touch is sending hot flashes to every available synapse, and it takes everything I've got not to shove her to the floor and get on with what I was dreaming about half the night. "No blow jobs. What're you looking for?"

"Something for breakfast."

"Never mind Marshall's whole wheat toast and natural peanut butter." She pats my back and then straightens. "I'll take you out for breakfast."

I am all too eager to get out of the house and into the safety of the day. We get on the bus and take two seats side by side, which I can honestly say I haven't done since I was a kid and my mom made me sit beside her. We don't talk much on the bus. We've never hung out outside of Harbor House, so maybe she's as weirded out about it as I am. In the heart of the Downtown Eastside, with the downtown core and its high-rise gloss and efficient bustle only ten blocks away, she pulls the cord for the bus to stop.

"What's here?" I say with venom.

She grabs my hand and pulls me out of the seat. "Only the best breakfast in the city."

We cross the street against traffic in the middle of the block, like everyone else does down here, and walk another half a block until we're standing in front of the Ovaltine Café. I'm not sure what we're doing is a date or just two wards of the state killing time, but because it might be a date, I don't want to be a freak and tell her I don't go to the Ovaltine. Not anymore. In fact, I haven't set foot in it since that day ten years ago.

Chapter Thirteen

"Where your mom?" the grandmotherly Chinese lady who runs the Ovaltine asks me. She had just rushed out onto the street and stopped me, clamping her hand on my bare shoulder. "Why you alone? Where Ella?" I'm in my pajamas... the ones with the fire trucks and Dalmatian dogs. This lady always scares me. She's nice to me, always telling me to call her Popo, but she has long red nails and arching penciled eyebrows and a wart that makes her look like a witch. My mom's name is not Ella. She only calls herself that on

the street, after Ella Fitzgerald. "Fitzgerald was going to be your middle name," she sometimes tells me when we're listening to her singing. "Or Ella, if you were a girl." Sometimes the songs are cheerful, but sometimes they are sad. The Chinese lady shakes my shoulder. "You too young to be out by yourself. You come in. I give you hot chocolate, okay?"

"Ethan?" Kelly is pumping my hand like we're a couple of businessmen meeting for the first time. "Hey!"

"Yeah?"

"You totally spaced out."

I swallow the lump of panic in my throat. It's just a dingy old café. I glance up at the neon sign. I used to love seeing it when I was really little, after my mom and I came back from visiting her brother in Wetaskiwin. The Greyhound would drive right past it on the way to the station. Sometimes they'd let us off on this corner, if the driver was nice, but usually he'd make us ride all the way to the station, and then we'd have to walk back. If it was open, we'd go in for hot chocolate and a plate of fries.

I shove aside the past and boldly push open the door and let Kelly go in ahead of me. The same Chinese lady greets us with a frown. I know it's her. Older, but still with the fingernails and freaky penciled eyebrows. She doesn't look at me, just shuffles past us, dropping off menus on her way.

"I love the pancakes here," Kelly's saying. I try to focus on her voice. The woman comes back and fills our mugs with lukewarm coffee.

"You order food too," she barks. "Not just coffee."

We both order the pancakes, which seems to satisfy her. She brings the bill with the food and then takes her seat at the front booth, opens her Chinese paper and lights a cigarette.

Chapter Fourteen

After breakfast we walk along Hastings toward the movie theater at the far edge of the Downtown Eastside.

"You don't like pancakes?" Kelly says, sauntering past two drug dealers right up in each other's face, screaming at the top of their lungs, fists clenched. When I was a little kid living down here, that stuff didn't bother me either, but now it makes me nervous. "You hardly touched them."

"I wasn't as hungry as I thought," I mutter. Instinctively I put my hand around Kelly's waist and pull her a little closer as a knot of junkies slither by, all jerky motions and full of twitch.

"Hey." She removes my hand. "I can take care of myself, thanks."

So I guess this isn't a date.

"Sure." I stick my hands in my pockets to avoid touching her again. "But if something happens, who do you think has to defend your honor?"

"My honor?" She fixes me with a sideways look. "My *honor*?"

"I'm no psychic…" I look her up and down, raising my eyebrows at her slip of a sundress and knee-high boots with the heels that make her almost as tall as me, and she is a short little bit of a girl when she's barefoot. "But even I can predict someone's going to want a piece of you down here, whether they have to pay for it or not."

"Really. Huh." Kelly plants her hands on her hips and stops in her tracks. "Look, Ethan, you might've grown up in this hellhole, but I've spent my fair share of time down here too. I know a thing or two about surviving, so don't go thinking you're going to be my knight in shining armor, because, frankly, I doubt you could 'defend my honor' without getting yourself killed."

I don't care about her slagging me off, not at all. All I want to know is how she knows I used to live down here.

"Who told you that?"

"Harvir. So what?" She starts walking again. "You think you've got this whole aloof 'I'm so tortured you can't touch me with a ten-foot pole' thing going on, but you're no more special or screwed up than the rest of us inmates, Ethan."

"What'd he say about it? What'd Harvir tell you?"

She stops again, turning with a flourish that spins her dress out as if she was a model turning at the end of the runway. "Are you even listening to me?"

"What'd Harvir say?"

Other than the art therapist, Harvir is the only one I've told the whole story to. He promised he wouldn't tell anyone, *ever*. Sure, other people know because the art therapist had to tell the social workers and police, but Harvir is the only other real person I've ever told.

"Just that you lived down here!" Kelly's shouting now. "You're being such a freak. What is your problem?"

He didn't tell her the rest? He didn't tell her more? "Is that all he said?"

"You know what?" Kelly holds up her hands and starts backing away. "Forget the movie. You're on your own."

"Wait!" I shake my head, trying to dislodge the headache that's digging in deeper. "Kelly, I'm sorry! Wait up!" I don't want her to go. I don't want to be left alone down here. Even though I'm taller and stronger than she is, even though I'm the guy and I should be doing the protecting, I don't want to let her go. I don't want to be alone. She lets me catch up to her and we keep walking, neither of us saying anything.

We get smuggled into the theater by her friend, who is a janitor for the shopping complex. When it's over and we leave, the sunshine of the afternoon is like a slap in the face. Kelly marches back toward Main and Hastings. I decide it's time for a peace offering.

"Pain and Wastings," I tell her as we approach

the corner. "That's what we call it down here."
Before I can correct the *we* to *they,* Kelly pipes
up.

"Look." She roots in her enormous purse for
a cigarette. "I'm going to score. I understand if
you don't want to. I know you think I'm just
some junkie skank. But there it is. That's what
I'm going to do with the rest of my afternoon,
okay?" She pulls out three packs, but they're
all empty. Barely missing a beat, she sidles up
to a group of men who are walking hurriedly
and speaking Italian, clearly tourists who got
dangerously lost trying to get from Chinatown
to the harbor.

They are all young and they are all quite
taken by Kelly. Four cigarettes are whipped
out. She slips the first one between her lips and
lets the man light it for her. Then she takes the
other three and tucks them into one of the empty
cigarette packs.

"*Gracias*," she purrs. They laugh and start
on their way again. She walks with them. They
don't seem to mind. My back goes up. I want to
pull her away, but this is Kelly. You don't mess
with her or she might knock you over with her

purse and stomp your eye out with one of her high heels.

She's not your girlfriend, I tell myself as one of the men puts his arm around her waist, and the balding one lays claim to her shoulders. She looks tiny between them.

"See you later, Ethan." She offers a little wave over her shoulder, leaving me utterly alone at the corner of Pain and Wastings.

"Where you headed, little guy?" I know this man. He is called Clifford and has red hair and is big, just like the big red dog in the picturebooks. This is before the Ovaltine, but the same day, only minutes earlier. I am clumping along with my snow boots on the wrong feet, my bare chest cold. It is fall and sunny, but colder than I expected.

"I'm getting milk," I tell him.

"Where's your mom?" He leans down. He reaches into his pocket and offers me a caramel, sticky and squished. I know it is safe to take candy from him because Mommy always lets me. I take it and turn my attention to peeling off the wrapper. That takes too long, and I am too hungry and this is the first thing in who knows

*how long that I've been offered to eat. I shove
the whole thing in my mouth and take off at a run
when I see the hand signal says it's safe to cross.
I want to get away from him before he asks me
where my mother is again. "Wait up, Ethan!"
Clifford calls after me. But he has a limp and
can't walk fast, so I'm across the street before he
starts after me, and then the light changes and
he has to wait.*

I manage to get on a bus out of the Downtown
Eastside. I should never have left the house this
morning. I'm not sure if I want anyone to be
home when I get there or not. Unless it is Harvir.
I wish he were there. I wish I had someone to talk
to. I'm not mad at him for what he said to Kelly.
So long as that's all he told her.

    When I get off the bus, I spot a penny in
the street. I pick it up and make a wish to find
Harvir up in our room, reading his East Indian
comics and smoking against the rules, aiming the
evidence out the window.

    Maybe I am going crazy. Maybe this is the
beginning. Before Tyrone moved in, Marshall sat
us all down and explained about schizophrenia

and what it does to your brain and how it can usually be managed by medication. He told us it often presents in the teenage years but isn't usually diagnosed until later. He said there is sometimes a family link, which is why Tyrone has the diagnosis already. His mom had it and couldn't take care of him.

Did my mom have it? Do I? There's no way of finding out about her. Her brother died four years ago, and I don't know how to get in contact with any of the rest of her family, and neither does Chandra. When my mom got really drunk and put on her sad music, full of mournful saxophones and deep bluesy voices, she would sometimes tell me about her dad. He was a musician, but that's pretty much all I know.

All of this started with Holly. She's like some dark angel making me relive all this stuff. Maybe I'll bail on the last two shifts. Juvie would be better than this hell.

But then Chandra's outside, honking her horn. I pull the clothes from the dryer, put them on damp and run out to her car. I'll do tonight and then I'll decide.

Before I even get there, I am angry at Holly. I *do* want to know how she knew my mother. Was she one of the paramedics who came in the end? Or did she pick her up one of the other times, when she overdosed, or when she was flopping on the floor, seizuring from some bad heroin? I knew how to call 911, but we rarely had a phone. So if I got scared, I'd go into the hallway and just start screaming at the top of my lungs until I got someone's attention.

The art therapist asked me why I didn't do that in the end. I remember staring at my painting on the easel in front of me. It was of the inside of the front door, with its three locks and peephole and the pictures of jazz greats Mom taped up there, although you couldn't tell who they were in my rendition. They were just blobs.

"Can you tell me why that time was different, Ethan?" Marigold asks.

Ages ago, at our first session, she told me her name. Marigold, like the flower. She must've guessed by my expression that I didn't know what a marigold looked like, so she led me to a pot of them in a square of sunlight and let me stand there quietly staring at them until I was ready to begin.

"It's okay to tell me what was different about that time." Now it was almost a year and two foster homes since I had started seeing her. "Take your time."

"It was different," I told her, "because the door was locked way up high." I pointed to the highest lock in the picture. "And that one needed a key."

"I wonder then," she said gently, "how you got out. Remember when they found you wandering around in your pajamas?"

I didn't tell her the whole story that time. I clammed up, like I usually did. I fixed my sights on the marigolds at the windowsill and didn't pick up another pencil or crayon or paintbrush for the rest of the hour.

Chapter Fifteen

The memories are coming back more than I would ever wish them to. The smells, the flies. The hunger. I stumble through the nightshift making stupid mistakes. Holly yells at me when I admit that I left the oxygen tank up in some old folks' home hallway after we were all the way to the hospital. We had to tell dispatch that we had to go back. There were calls waiting. They were pissed off.

"I told you to get some sleep!" she snaps at five in the morning when I drop the burns kit, sending the sterile gauze and saline tumbling under the ambulance. "You're lucky it's packaged so well or I'd really be mad." She collects what she needs and tells me to pick up the rest. She goes inside to where John is trying to calm the little kid who pulled the pot of hot water onto himself off the stove. I trail inside, exhausted. My limbs are heavy, and the short slices of sleep I got on the station couch in the downtime make me feel worse than if I hadn't slept at all. The mother is bawling.

"It's not as bad as it could've been," Holly is saying. The mother is holding the child still while John dumps another liter of saline over the pink blotch on the kid's belly. He's about three, dark skinned, which makes the pink look kind of odd.

"I was getting my husband his breakfast," the mother says. Her accent is thick, Middle Eastern maybe. The husband is standing near the door in oily coveralls, gripping a lunchbox. He looks crestfallen, as if it were all his fault. You can tell he's not sure if he should risk being late for work, or if he should leave now and break his little boy's heart.

"Daddy!" the boy wails. He reaches out. "Daddy!"

The father drops his lunchbox and gets down on his knee beside the boy. "It's okay, Amir. You no worry," he says in faltering English. "I stay for you, son." Then he switches to his mother tongue, murmuring into the boy's ear as he strokes his hair. There are several other people lurking in the dim light of dawn. A set of grandparents sitting quietly at the table, eyes full of concern. Two older sisters in matching pink nighties. Another much older man, maybe a great-uncle or another grandfather. This boy is so loved it makes me hate him. I am jealous.

As we pull away with the son sitting in his father's lap on the cot, the whole family comes out to see him off. The mother is crying, a daughter clinging to each arm. The others are consoling her. The boy has stopped bawling. He sniffs back more tears, his nose dripping with snot. His father wipes at it with a handkerchief he takes from his coveralls. Holly offers him one of the bears they keep to give to kids. Amir clutches it to his chest and whispers a shy thank-you in English when his father prompts him to.

I am full of envy. And so mad I cannot utter one word for fear that I will let loose all of the wicked thoughts in my head. Where was everyone when I was his age? Why didn't anyone look after me? How could they have not come for me? Why didn't anyone know what had happened?

I don't say a word as we make our way back to the station after dropping little Amir and his father off at the children's hospital. I slam out of the back of the ambulance and stalk into the station to splash my face with cold water in the bathroom. When I've taken as much time in there as I can without drawing attention, I head back out to the bay to help Holly and John clean up the car.

"You better be more on your game tonight," Holly says as we heave a new main oxygen tank into its cabinet. "I don't know what your problem is, but you were about as useful as a tit on a bull all night."

"I think you know exactly what my problem is," I growl as we wedge the heavy tank into place.

"You want to talk about it, I'm right here," she says. Her words are sharp, like she's frustrated, or pissed off, I'm not sure. "We've been dancing around the issue for three shifts now, and I've been really good about it, leaving it up to you if you want to talk about it. I'm not going to press. You're not six years old anymore."

I slam the cabinet shut. I ball up my fists and eye the fiberglass door of the supply shelves. I want to punch something so bad I can feel my muscles tightening in anticipation. Instead I back out of the ambulance and trip on the last step. I land on my back, my head cracking on the cement floor.

"What the hell do you want?" I put a hand to my head and then the other one too. I grip my head and yell the words at her again. "What the hell do you want from me?"

John pops his head out of the stockroom and catches Holly's eye. "Everything okay?"

"Yeah," Holly says. She climbs out of the ambulance and offers me a hand up. "Want some ice for that?"

"Leave me alone!" I twist away and turn onto my knees. I stand, my head pounding.

"Are you going to be okay?"

"What the hell do you care?" I grab my backpack and take off out into the morning. It's only 6:00 AM, but already it's bright and getting warm, as if spring is putting extra effort into this day. I head up to Hastings and turn east. About five minutes later, I hear Holly's car clunk down into first gear beside me. There's no way I'll replace her clutch now. She's a bitch. She's toying with me. Like this is some warped version of *A Christmas Carol* and she is the ghost of dead mothers past.

"Want a ride?"

She was going to drive me home, which is why I don't have any money for a cab or bus. I shake my head, refusing to look at her. Why? Not because I'm afraid I might reach through the open window and throttle her or hit her or something. The urge to swing at something has vanished. If I look at her now, I might cry. I clench my jaw and keep walking. "No thanks," I say.

"Suit yourself," she says and wrenches the clutch into second. The car lurches off just in time. I start crying. I'm at the overpass above the train tracks. I turn away from the slow-moving slug of commuter traffic oozing into the city and grip the railing. I could be over it in one hop. What would go through my mind in the seconds between jumping and splatting open on the tracks far below? Would thoughts of my mother finally go away? Or is that all I would think about? I push my weight onto the balls of my feet, testing the effort it would take to throw myself over.

There are a couple of tarps set up under the overpass. An old man crawls out from one. He's wearing one-piece underwear, like in the olden days. He puts his hands to the small of his back and stretches, letting loose a great bellow of a yawn. He sees me at the railing and waves.

"Top of the morning to you," he yells. "Beautiful day!"

I lift my hand in an empty greeting and then take off at a run. If I do go ahead and kill myself, I'll do it on Holly's shift so maybe she'd be the one to have to scrape my brains off the train tracks. It'd serve her right.

I'm not a pussy. The crying is just because I'm tired. It can get to you. I am *not* a pussy. I'll do the last nightshift because I *can*. I'm strong enough, and it's true: I'm not six anymore. I'll do it and then I will walk away and never set foot in the Downtown Eastside again. A last good-bye to Holly, and she's gone from my life. I know how that goes. It's not hard to say good-bye. I've had fourteen foster moms and lived as a citizen in a nation of ever-rotating foster "brothers" and "sisters." The easy part is saying good-bye.

Chapter Sixteen

An unmistakable, high-pitched scream from Kelly wakes me up that afternoon. I poke my head out into the hallway and see her knee-deep in her crap in her room at the end. She's hurling things out at Marshall, who is leaning—weary with red-rimmed eyes and a look like he's about to break into a yawn at any moment—against the banister.

"Hissy fit," he reports when he sees me. "Sorry to wake you."

Rubbing the sleep from my eyes, I shuffle

toward her room. "What's going on, Kelly?" I stay in the hallway as she launches a high-heeled missile at me.

"Detox, that's what!" She scoops the contents of her makeup drawer into a ratty travel case.

"Where you will not need your makeup," Marshall says. "Nor will it be allowed."

She drops everything to lock a furious glare on him. "*What*?"

He repeats himself. She does not break her stare. He says it again, this time in pig Latin, which just infuriates her more.

"You're making fun of me!"

"They're coming for you in fifteen minutes, princess," Marshall says as she throws a tampon at him. "Thank you." He picks it up and pockets it. "How ever did you know it was my time of the month?"

"Because you're being such a bitch," she says to him as she marches to the door and pulls me into her room. "God!" She slams it in his face. "What an asshole."

Boys are not allowed in her and Nikki's room. I wait for the knock on the door, the order to get out, but either Marshall can't be bothered to enforce the rule right this second, or he's not too worried about what we can get up to in fifteen minutes.

Kelly plops herself down on the mess that is her bed. With a sigh, she upends the makeup case and runs her hands over the compacts and tubes and sticks. She picks up a plum-colored gloss and calmly dabs it on.

"What'd you get up to yesterday?" she asks with a smack of her lips.

"After you went off with those four creepy men, you mean?" I back up to the wall and snug myself against it. I've never set foot in here before, so I'm not sure what to do with myself. Nikki's side of the room is, not surprisingly, flying the Goth national colors of black and more black, but Kelly's side is overwhelmingly *girly*. Peach curtains, a white trundle bed, a flowery scarf draped over her bedside lamp. And it smells like her, of perfume and lingering cigarettes. Sweet and smoky.

"We hung out. I went to their hotel room." She drops the gloss and picks up a tube of mascara. "Jacuzzi tub. Room service. Very swank."

"How much did they pay you?"

She looks up from the little mirror she's using, the mascara wand poised at her lashes. "None of your business."

Except for her teeth, she is so achingly beautiful, I just want to lock her in this room forever, or at least until she realizes how uncool it is to be a sixteen-year-old meth addict who turns tricks to fund her habit.

"Detox will be really good for you," I say.

"What the hell do you know about it?"

"Enough." I went with my mom to a First Nations detox center on an island off the north coast when I was five. We took a floatplane, and then a boat took us the rest of the way. We were there for a month. My mom slept in the bottom bunk, and I got the top. Every morning I joined the other children for lessons in the little schoolroom, and in the afternoon we played games. I doubted the concrete block Kelly was heading to was anything like that.

"Come here," Kelly says.

"Why?"

She caps the mascara and tosses it aside. "Just get over here."

I take a step forward.

She's staring at me, waiting for me to come closer. "Oh, never mind."

I'm thinking I'm off the hook, but then she launches herself off the bed and grabs me. She spins us around and shoves me onto the bed and straddles me. With her arms above my head, she leans in and kisses me. Grape lip-gloss and peppermint gum and the hint of her last cigarette. That's all I taste, not the rot of her teeth, which I was afraid of, to be honest. Her lips are soft, slightly sticky from the gloss, and her tongue is determined. She parts my lips with hers and wiggles her hips.

"Kelly—" I groan as she moves one hand to my waist. "I don't think we—"

"Come on," she murmurs in my ear. "You're dying to."

A honk sounds from out in front of the house. Footsteps on the stairs. Marshall's voice in the hall. A knock on the door. "Your chariot awaits, princess."

Kelly kisses me again, hard. "Thanks, Marsh," she says to the door.

I am lying on the bed, unable to move, while she throws the last few things into her pack. All of a sudden she's in a much better mood. I, however, have been paralyzed. I can't see myself leaving this spot until she is able to resume her position and continue where we left off.

"Tell him to wait five minutes," I plead when it's clear she's about to leave. "Come on, Kelly. Tell them you're not dressed."

Backpack over one shoulder, she climbs on me again, but only long enough to squeeze me through my jeans and give me a French kiss for the road.

"I'll be back," she whispers in my ear. "They're going to fix my teeth while I'm in there. That's reason enough to go." She climbs off and straightens her skirt. "I was going to run away, but I figure I might as well get them fixed."

And then she is gone.

Chapter Seventeen

Chandra picks me up at five thirty to drive me to the station one last time.

"Enjoying it so far?" she asks.

I don't want to get into it, so I nod.

But she persists. "What do you like the best?"

"Hmm." I hold my hands out, comparing invisible weights. "Either the stench of piss and vomit or the constant reminder of my dead mother. Not sure. It's a toss-up."

Chandra doesn't rise to the bait. She lets

out a prim little sigh and signals to turn onto Cordova.

"Do I have to go to school tomorrow?" I ask her as I get out of the car, my paper-bag lunch in one hand, backpack in the other, like she's my mother dropping me off at a sleepover.

"Of course not," she says. "You'll have to get some sleep."

"That's right." My mood brightens. "Yes, I'll be *far* too tired to go to school tomorrow. Must recover from grueling nightshift."

"Captain will expect you on Friday. He'll want your essay."

"Essay?"

"Yes, essay." Another stuck-up little sigh. She is not in a good mood today. "The one you were clearly told that Captain wanted to see at the end of your block of shifts. Five hundred words."

"On what?"

"What do you think?" A bigger sigh now. "Ethan, I'd hoped this experience might help you deal with certain aspects of your life story."

"Here we go." I back away from the car.

"Was I wrong?" She stretches across the front seat to talk out the open door at me. "I meant well. I thought you might benefit from a chance to revisit the area, but safely this time, grown up enough to put things into perspective instead of always having them as the larger-than-life demons they've been for you."

"It was all better left forgotten." I suddenly feel like I'm the adult and Chandra is the one in trouble. If I was a different kid I might think to write her up about this stupid stunt. This is the kind of thing social workers actually get in trouble for. *A poor decision, which forced me to relive deeply traumatizing aspects of my difficult childhood*...That sort of thing.

"We'll talk." She says this more softly. "Tomorrow, after you've slept. Okay?"

I shrug.

"Just get through tonight, okay?" She flutters something at me. "Here."

"What's that?"

"You might want it. You might not."

It's a sticky note with an address written on it. Reading the numbers sends a chill down my spine. I feel the grilled cheese sandwich Marshall made me eat before I left threaten to resurface. I look up from the paper. Chandra has gotten out of her car and is standing beside me, reaching to take it back. "It's a mistake. Sorry. Bad idea. I honestly thought maybe enough time had passed. I was wrong. I apologize."

"You go to school for this?" I shove the paper in my pocket. "So I could go to university for four years and get a degree like you and be some kid's social worker forever and then turn around and dig a big knife into his back? That's in your job description?"

"I said I was sorry. Look, if you want to cancel today, I'd understand. We'll call it even."

"Go home, Chandra." I back away, daring her to follow. She doesn't, and for that I am proud of her. "Go home to your husband and daughter and have supper and give her a bath and put her to bed. Maybe you could tell her a bedtime story. Maybe the one about the little boy stuck in an apartment with his dead mother for a week. It has a happy ending, or so they claim."

I turn and bang on the locked door of the station. John opens it. He frowns when he sees me. I'm guessing I look kind of grim.

"Are you all right?"

"Let's just get this over with, okay?"

"Sure." He half smiles and opens the door wider. "That's what we all say on our last nightshift. Come on in."

Now that it's my last shift, I'm finally getting used to the paramedic thing. Get the call, find the address, lights and sirens on the way there, or not, depending on the emergency. Find the patient, ask the questions, load them up. Go. And in there somewhere, there might be a splint to put on, medicine to deliver, even CPR to do, but every call uses the same pattern. I could actually see Kelly being good at this. As much as her life seems to be chaotic, she likes structure. And along with the structure, there is the freedom of the job. Just you and your partner running the show, unless you have some kid riding along with a great big chip on his shoulder, like me.

I'm leaning against the wall in a fusty hallway of yet another three-story walk-up rooming house, holding on to the chair cot, waiting to be called in to set it up. It's a contraption to carry people downstairs when there's no elevator or it's busted or the stretcher doesn't fit in the puny elevator there is.

Holly comes out. "Only wants John to touch him. Fine by me."

She looks at the wall. "That thing's filthy. I wouldn't lean against it if I were you."

Instead of engaging in her attempts at casual conversation—which I've been ignoring since the shift started—I pull the sticky note out of my pocket and stick it to her name badge. After a pause, she plucks it off and stares at it.

"I know the address," she says. "We go there all the time."

"Did you go there ten years ago?" I don't look at her when I ask it because I'm not sure I want to know. But I can't go on like this, the tension pulling so tight that I'm considering various means of killing myself just to make it ease.

"Sure," she says. She lights a cigarette. I've never seen her do that before, light one during a call. Usually she waits and sneaks one behind the hospital with the other paramedic smokers. She takes a long drag off it and then nods. "I've been working down here for fourteen years."

All of a sudden it becomes easier just to ask it than to hold it in anymore. "Is that how you knew my mom?"

"Nope."

This startles me. I had already decided that must be how she knew my mom.

"Then how?"

"Narcotics Anonymous." A tap of the ash.

"Oh." I don't know what to say. I was so sure she had something to do with what happened. I try to rearrange my anger into something less loaded.

"That's where I met her first. You were just a baby. She was trying to get you back from the courts, and going to NA was one of the things they wanted her to do."

"You were in NA?"

"Still am." A big grin. "Seventeen years clean."

John calls for us from inside the guy's room. Holly stubs out her cigarette.

"Did you know her when…I mean, just before?"

"I hadn't seen her in a while," she says softly and takes a step inside the room. "Later, okay?"

Chapter Eighteen

At first I thought she was asleep, and then I thought she'd overdosed. I knew about that. She'd done it before. But this time was different. The man had finished, zipped up his pants and had a drink of water she offered him in the coffee mug with her real name on it. Christina. They murmured back and forth for a bit, and then their voices got louder and he told her she wasn't worth a penny let alone the price she was asking. And then he hit her, and she fell and he kept on hitting her. I was in the closet by the

*front door where she tucked me when she had
no other option but to bring them home. I heard
him punching her. She made little "ooph, ooph"
sounds. She didn't scream, not once. Sometimes I
think it's because she didn't want me to be afraid.
Maybe she thought he would leave, and I would
run into the hall and scream for help. Like the
other times we needed help. When he was finished
with her, he opened the closet, almost like an
afterthought, and found me there.*

*He took a stick of gum from his pocket and
offered it to me. He held his fingers to his lips
and said, "Shhhh." And then he climbed out the
window and left by the fire escape. I sat beside
my mother in the bathroom, her head bloody, one
hand reaching for the shower stall, like all she
wanted was to rinse him off.*

I go through the rest of that night in a haze. We
are out until 5:00 AM, dealing with assaults and
sick people, little old ladies with chest pain, an
old man who passed out during an all-night game
of mah jong in a storefront in Chinatown.

"Any pain?" Holly asks, pointing to various
places. Head, heart, gut. "*Tong ma?*"

I want to answer in his place. Yes, pain. I have pain in all those places. Head, heart. Gut. I want to ask her more about my mother, but our night is so busy that we don't get a chance to eat, let alone sit for a minute and talk about my mother. I want to hear what she has to say now, and now that I am willing to hear it, we can't get a second of quiet.

We go back to the station at 5:00 AM, only to be called out again ten minutes later for a car accident at Main and Hastings.

Pain and Wastings.

We careen around the corner and stop off to the side of the crash. A motorcycle had been going straight through the green light when a cargo van turned left in front of him. The biker plowed into the side of the van and flew another thirty feet, landing in a crumpled heap in the middle of the road. His motorcycle is totaled. His helmet is cracked in four places, and he is unconscious.

"Get the spine board," Holly orders as we get out of the ambulance. "And collar kit."

I collect both from the cubby at the back and run to her side. A fireman is already holding the guy's head steady as he sucks in irregular gasps. John thrusts his cut-all scissors at me and tells me to cut off the man's leather jacket while he puts on the hard collar.

"Don't jostle him!" Collar on, John lines himself up beside the fireman to orchestrate the roll that will get the man onto the spine board.

The man comes to as I am cutting through his jacket. "Brand-new…" he blurts through a mouthful of blood. "Bastard…" He gurgles something more, but I can't make out what it is.

"Sorry, sir." I slice neatly down one arm, then the other. Up one pant leg, down the other. Both his femurs are busted—that's the thighbone. I only learned the word yesterday. Several firemen are holding him in place, bracing the fractures, while Holly has a listen to his chest with her stethoscope.

"Decreased breath sounds left side. Let's make it quick, guys. On three—" They roll him onto the board and lift him onto the cot. Another ambulance shows up. One of their crew joins Holly in the back as they set up for an iv line.

I'm not sure if I should maybe ride up front this time, but then Holly waves for me to get on board, and we take off for the hospital with the sirens blasting and lights all lit up. I cut off the rest of his clothes. When I peel off the last piece of his jeans, I see a white waxy burn along his lower leg. Pink is good in a burn. White is not. Holly told me that after the call with Amir.

"Did you see this?" I say to Holly.

"No." She glances at it, delegates the other paramedic to douse it with saline and put a sterile dressing on it. "Good job, Ethan. Thanks."

We cinch up the spider straps that hold him to the board, and then Holly hands me the man's wallet and tells me to find out his name.

I find his driver's license.

"Hey, Reginald!" I lean over him. "That your name?"

"Reggie," he coughs out with a mouthful of blood.

We're at the hospital now. They're waiting for us in the bay. We pull out the cot, and the emergency room team grabs on to one end of it. John pushes, and Holly jogs alongside, giving them the details as they wheel out of sight into the trauma room.

Of all four shifts, that was the best call. I feel alive and useful and puffed up with ability, like there is work to be done and I can do it. I am practically flying when we leave the hospital. It's almost 7:00 AM, the shift long over, so dispatch lets us go back to the station to switch crew. For the last hour and a bit, I'd forgotten all about my dead mother.

"So now you understand the term adrenalin junkie?" Holly laughs at me as I bounce around the station, going over the call.

"We might even miss you," John says, and then he and Holly both shake their heads and go, "No, we won't."

But they invite me back any time. I tell them about Kelly, and they say they'll see if she can do a ride-along too, so long as she sticks it out at detox first.

When I get into Holly's car, I tell her I can put in a new clutch for her. She cranks it into gear and says she'll think about it. And then I remember that we were going to talk about my mom. It's "later" now.

"Still want to?" she says, as if reading my mind. "Up to you."

"I guess so." I do want to know. I am curious. Despite everything. Despite trying to push it all away for so long. "Yes."

"Okay."

"Do you have time now?" We're at the light at Main and Hastings. "Or do you have to head straight home?"

"Sleep can wait."

"Can we go there?"

"Sure, Ethan." She turns right instead of left. She knows where I mean. She still has the sticky note somewhere, but I don't need the address written down to remember it and neither does she.

We pull up out front of the squat red-brick building. It was the best place we lived in down here. It had its own bathroom and a little kitchenette. It was still only a bachelor, but it felt enormous compared to the other places we lived.

"You think we can get in?"

"Sure." Holly is still wearing her uniform. We get out and carefully lock the car. This is the rougher end of the roughest part of the city and the poorest neighborhood in the whole country.

Someone is curled up in the doorway on a square of cardboard. Several earnest drinkers are already into the rice wine in the concrete park across the street. Holly pushes the buzzer marked *Manager*.

After two tries, we're let in by a very grumpy but obliging woman in a housecoat and slippers, her thin hair in three drooping rows of curlers. Is this the same woman who ran the building when we lived here? I frown at her, studying her features, trying to remember, but being inside the building is like being in a dream. Or a nightmare. The edges of my vision become fuzzy, and the present is slipping away, no matter how hard I clench my fists around it.

I was eleven and a half by the time I told Marigold how I got out. Five years after it happened.

"Everyone's always wondered how you got out, Ethan. When you didn't have the key for that upper lock."

"Same way he did," I said.

"How's that?"

"He came back and opened the door," I said matter-of-factly. "The key was hung up and I couldn't reach it. But he could."

If she was surprised, she did an amazing job of not showing it. "Wow. That was nice of him."

"He's not nice at all." I scratched out the frog I was drawing, covering it in black marker.

"You're right, Ethan. He's not." She slid a fresh piece of paper in front of me. "Do you want to tell me more?"

Chapter Nineteen

Holly asks the woman if there is an empty apartment, one we could just have a quick peek at. The woman eyes the two of us, takes another look at Holly's paramedic uniform and heads off down the hall. We follow her. She stops at her suite to collect a ring of keys.

"What do you want to look at it for?" she asks, with a grunt for the question mark.

"I used to live here," I say, not giving Holly the chance to make something up.

"You did not," the woman says firmly. "I'd know. Been here twenty years."

I remember her name all of a sudden. "Delores, right?"

She hesitates in her search for the right key. We're standing at the back on the second floor. My mom and I lived exactly one floor up.

"That's right," she finally says. And then, as she's fitting the key in the lock, "I know who you are. I know you. You're Christine's boy."

She opens the door and shuffles away before I can say anything else.

"Thank you," Holly calls after her.

I step inside the dim front hallway. Kitchenette to the right, bathroom to the left. Closet. And then the rest of the room, with only the one window at the back. Exact same layout.

"You okay?" Holly hangs back at the door. "Want me to leave you alone?"

"No!" I didn't mean it to come out so desperate, but I am. I don't want her to leave. I open the closet. It seems so small, but I remember it being much bigger. My mom used to lay out a sleeping bag with a flashlight under the pillow and all the stuffies I wanted to keep me company.

It was the closest thing to a bedroom I ever had. I loved it.

"I'm right here," Holly says. She lights a cigarette and moves into the kitchen so she can tap her ash into the sink.

"How much do you know?" I ask.

"All of it."

"Tell me."

"How much do you know?" she counters as if she is considering what to tell me.

"I was here." I point into the open closet. "Right here. There's nothing you can tell me that I don't already know." In my head or heart. Or gut.

"Your mom's name was Christine," Holly starts. "But she was called Ella on the streets. She was an amazing singer. She could sound just like Ella Fitzgerald one night and Nina Simone the next. She was amazing. So talented. I'd go watch her sometimes at the Honey Lounge. She was like something out of another era, you know? With beautiful dresses and her hair swept up. She was native—Mi'kmaq—you'd know that, of course, and she had this beautiful long black hair that went down to her waist. Do you remember that?"

I nod. "Go on." I open the bathroom door and see her there, black hair matted with blood, her body naked and splotchy with bruises. I blink. The vision vanishes.

"And then it turned into the same story of so many of the girls down here. She got into heroin, started turning tricks to pay for it. You came along. She cleaned herself up for a year or so and then slid back down."

"She was only half Mi'kmaq," I say. "Her father was African American. From South Carolina. A blues musician."

"I didn't know that."

"Want me to tell you the rest?" I ask.

After a pause, Holly nods. "Sure. If you want to."

"She brought this guy home. Big, tall, with a beard. They did their thing. Then he beat her up and left her for dead. I was right here." I turn and point at the closet again. "I saw the whole thing. He found me after. And then he left out the fire escape. He gave me a stick of gum and left. Maybe he thought I could undo the locks. Maybe he didn't bother to check if the door was locked. Maybe he didn't care, or maybe he got off on the idea of me starving to death with my dead mom to keep me company. I don't know."

"But he came back," Holly says. "I remember that."

I cross the room to the window, prop it open and lean out. I twist and look up. Right above. That's where it happened. We lived right up there.

"They figure it was a week or so later," I say. "I'd eaten everything in the place, which wasn't much. Even dried pasta and a jar of mustard. I remember that all I wanted was some milk. Ice-cold milk. Other than for my mom to wake up, that's all I wanted. When he came back through the window, I wasn't even surprised to see him. He threw up, because of the smell. Then he rushed to the front door, undid the three locks, cracked the door open and left again out the fire escape. He didn't say a word, not even one word."

"You think he felt guilty?" Holly lights another cigarette. "You think that's why he came back and let you out?"

I shrug. "I don't know."

"Seems so strange, that he'd come back a week later."

"Sometimes I think it was my mother haunting him, keeping him awake. Driving him crazy until he came back and made sure I'd gotten out."

After he left, I jammed my feet into my boots and stepped out into the hallway. I remember standing there for a moment, waiting for my mom to stop me. When she didn't, I headed down the stairs and outside. I was going to get some milk. I was going to bring it home and make her drink some and then maybe she would wake up. I smile now at my six-year-old logic. Dumb kid.

"I was working that day you showed up at the Ovaltine," Holly says. "I was the paramedic who checked you out."

I stare at her. I remember the bear. I remember being lifted into the back of the ambulance. I remember being tucked in a blanket, clutching that bear.

I remember something else too. Something new. "*You* bought me the carton of milk."

"That's right." Holly laughs, but it's a sad laugh. "And you said thank-you. And then I asked you your name and you told me. I hadn't seen you since you were a toddler, but I knew who you were. And I knew your mom was dead, or very sick, because you were in a terrible state."

"You probably thought she overdosed, right?"

She nodded, slowly. "When we found out she was murdered, we were all surprised."

Chapter Twenty

"What's your name, honey?" I am sitting in her lap, holding on to the bear she gave me. She's keeping the cops at a distance, tells the social worker to give me a minute.

"Ethan Mingus Kirby."

"Christine's boy?"

"Yeah. She's at home, but she's sick."

She nods. *"My name's Holly,"* she says as she waves over one of the cops. *"Can you tell us your address, Ethan Mingus Kirby the Brave?"*

I do know our address. My mom had me

*practice it. She says if I ever go to school, I'll
have to know things like that. For now, she
teaches me at home so they don't come snooping.
I'm not sure if it's okay to tell them my address,
but my mom is sick and bloody and she hasn't
moved in a lot of sleeps, and there are flies
buzzing around her and she smells bad and we
have nothing left to eat. I tell them about the flies
and the smell and the man who hurt her.*

*"Tell us your address, kid." The cop says
something into the radio. Another cop joins him
and they're both leaning into the back of the
ambulance, scaring me. I shake my head.*

*Holly cups her hand to my ear. "It's okay, you
can tell me. Me and your mom are friends."*

*So I tell her, and the cops write it down, and
they rush off and jump in their cruiser and take
off with the sirens screaming.*

Holly drives me home. When we get there, she
says she'll look into ordering the clutch for
me to put in. I say thanks, and I mean it in an
indescribably huge way, even though it's the
same small word we use all the time. She gives
me her cell number and tells me to call any

time, and it's not like when people say that and you know they don't mean it and you know you'll never call. I know I'll call. Maybe not right away. But I will. I want her to tell me more. About the nights she'd watch my mom sing. About the times when she was doing so good. About what changed, and how she slid back down again.

When Kelly comes home in a few weeks, I'll take her to the station so she can meet Holly and John. If she can leave her potty mouth and attitude at home, she might be able to ride along with them. I sleep for a few hours. When I wake up, I don't even leave my room to take a leak. I head straight for the little desk each of us has to encourage us to do our homework, and I start writing the five hundred words Captain wants from me. It turns into this, which is way bigger than five hundred words, in more ways than one.

Carrie Mac is a best-selling author in a number of genres. Her first novel, *The Beckoners*, won the Stellar Teen Award and the Arthur Ellis Award from Crime Writers of Canada. *Crush* and *Charmed*, both Orca Soundings novels, have been nominated for the American Library Association's Quick Picks list.

A paramedic, Carrie Mac lives near Whistler, British Columbia.